Fluff
In the Land of Unicorns

WRITTEN AND ILLUSTRATED BY
Mary I. Gomez-Winborne

To order additional copies of this book, contact:
Xlibris
1-888-795-4274
www.Xlibris.com
Orders@Xlibris.com

ISBN: 978-1-4568-6889-5 (sc)
ISBN: 978-1-4568-6962-5 (hc)
ISBN: 978-1-7960-9564-7 (e)

Print information available on the last page

Rev. date: 03/23/2020

For
Marty, Brian & Kevin
Also
Matthew and Diane

One day not very long ago, what was supposed to be an ordinary day for delivering babies, became a huge and very jumbled problem. Over 5000 storks were out sick with an unusual virus. They had to call forward all retired storks to help deliver babies. They even called forward the oldest stork Drabu, who had not made any kind of delivery in over 800 years. Now Drabu being very old had very bad eye sight, even with his glasses on. It did not help matters that his hearing was also nearly gone.

While everyone thought things were going quite well, no one knew Fluff being an overly curious and mischievous feline was about to get lost.

Fluff and her three brothers were being carried by none other than Old Drabu. So determined and anxious to see the world, Fluff stepped right on top of her brother's heads. Fluff Pushed and prodded until she could finally see outside the dropsac. Intrigued with the mountains and rivers, valleys and oceans and all the beauty of the world; she pushed forward even harder. Fluff almost fell from a 1000 feet in the air. Lucky for her Drabu was getting quite tired, so he touched down on an island to rest. As he sat perched on a big fat cushy mushroom, Drabu checked his directions. He wanted to make sure his bearings were correct.

Drabu never noticed Fluff tumbled out of the dropsac. As she tumbled she fell completely off of the mushroom. Before Fluff could climb back up the mushroom, Drabu assured of his bearings and somewhat rested took flight again. . Fluff sat watching Drabu fly away listening to her brothers all meowing at once. They were trying to tell Drabu that their sister was being left behind.

Drabu only smiled as he could faintly hear the meowing, he thought they must be hungry; so he tried to reassure them by saying "Don't worry kittens you'll be home soon."

Slowly Drabu and his cargo disappeared. Fluff gave out one last long pitiful meow and then she began to walk around checking her surroundings. She was almost dwarfed by the giant mushrooms. As she went through the mushroom forest she saw many kinds of plants and beautiful shiny rocks. There were flowers of ever size and color imaginable. She delighted in seeing the clouds lazily floating by make many kinds of shapes.

Fluff did not wander far, when she heard a deep odd voice behind her

"Haaaaallllttttt !!!! Whooooooooooooooo goes there?"

Fluff turned and stared into big yellow eyes watching her, she noticed this creature had a wide head, a short beak and was perched with huge talons holding onto the branch of a small tree. With the hair on her back straight up and the tingle of goose bumps everywhere, Fluff managed a very weak "H ...H.....Hello sir, I....I .....am Fluff."

"What are you doing here in Timboura? Where did you come from?" The creature

sounded so demanding.

"Well ... you see ....I was being delivered by Drabu ..... and when he landed on that mushroom over there. I kinda stumbled out of the dropsac an'............"

Before she could finish the creature began in a kinder voice "Drabu!! How can that be, why he delivered me more than 900 years ago. I thought he quit delivering several hundred years ago."

Fluff told the creature "Yes, well I'm not exactly sure sir; but I did hear that there was an awful virus that made many storks quite ill and.........."

"Yes ....oh my! Yes child, I think I understand, but it is of no consequence now. We have a very serious problem here. You see my dear, there are no cats here on Timboura so whatever will you do with yourself?"

Fluff "I...don't know sir ....Sir? Who are you?"

The creature gave out a big hoot and said "I'm sorry Miss, we both seem to have so many questions about each other. I seemed to have forgotten my manners! I apologize, am known as Sir Gahn, I am an owl and I live here on Timboura."

"Timboura?" Fluff repeated with a slight question in her voice.

"Yes my dear child this is Timboura it is the farthest corner of the Great Earth it is between somewhere and everywhere. This island is inhabited mainly by Unicorns, Sprites, Elves, Leprechaun, Fairies, many birds and a few other odd creatures of the earth. As far as I know child there never have been any of your species here."

Fluff cried out "Whatever shall I do Sir Gahn?"

"I wish I could answer that for you little one, but alas it is not for even a wise owl like me to phantom the answer to that question." Sir Gahn and Fluff silently stared at one another for a few moments, finally Sir Gahn continued "Listen very carefully to what I tell you Miss Fluff. You must stay right here in this very spot . Do not wander off. I will go and get my friend King Fiodoire, he is a unicorn and the King of Timboura. Once I've informed him about you, he will send me or another unicorn to come and get you."

"Why can't I just go with you now, Sir Gahn?"

"Because my child, since there are none of your kind here it might cause fear and much confusion. It is best that everyone be informed, before seeing you."

"Why............?

"Why? Why must you continue on so? Trust me child, it is for the best this way."

Slowly, deliberately, Fluff said "Sir Gahn? ....What is a unicorn?"

Ah yes ....you see child I am not as wise as I once was. Unicorns are graceful creatures, not much bigger than yourself. They too walk on four legs like yourself but have hooves instead of paws for feet. Unicorns each have a horn in the middle of their foreheads and they are the most loving and gentlest creatures on the Great Earth. However you must realize they live here apart from the rest of the world for good reason."

Sir Gahn continued, "Let me tell you how it came to pass that they should live here. Humans found that owning one of these creatures brought them prosperity and good fortune. Greed soon got in the way of reason, compassion or righteousness. Everyone began fighting for them, even killing for them. After many centuries of what once used to be great herds of unicorns, soon became almost an extinct species."

"Oh Sir Gahn that sounds terrible." Fluff said in amazement and sorrow.

"That it was. It wasn't just the unicorns that had this sort of trouble sprites, elves, leprechauns and fairies were also dying. One day a pelican told King Fiodoire about this island. Fiodoire wasn't a king then but it inspired him to call a great meeting with his fellow unicorns. At this meeting it was agreed that they would come and inhabit this island, which they later named Timboura. They named it Timboura because there are no great timber trees of any kind here. In the Leprechaun world any land with no timber is known as Timboura. Fiodoire talked the unicorns into offering refuge to all the others with similar problems.

At the second meeting with all the other creatures present, one of the elves stepped forward and declared "Hello, hello fellow residents and friends my name is Nivek. I hope that you will all agree with me that our beloved friend Fiodoire seems to be the wisest amongst us here tonight. Having found such an agreeable solutions for us all! I think we should here and now make him our king!" Not a single creature disagreed. From what I understand that as over 6000 years ago and to this day not one creature has found a single reason to change or regret their decision."

"Now Miss Fluff as I was saying before, we must decide what to do with you!"

Fluff sat on top of a large flower and agreed with the wise owl " Yes Sir Gahn, I will wait right here until you or someone comes for me. Please hurry cause I'm kind of scared."

Sir Gahn takes to the air and reassures the kitten, "Please try not to worry child, not a single creature on this island would hurt you . I will see you quite soon."

The coolness of the flower soothed Fluff and with a blink of an eye she soon fell fast asleep.

In Mangdu the Rainbow city of Timboura, Sir Gahn quickly tells King Fiodoire about the kitten, Drabu, and the problem they were facing.

After hearing the story presented by Sir Gahn, the King calls forth his daughter Pirsia "Daughter you heard Sir Gahn's story, you must go to where his perch is, on the out skirts of the mushroom forest. Find this kitten and bring her back to Mangdu tell her she will be our guest until we find a solution to her predicament. "

King Fiodoire turned to his friend Sir Gahn and said "You my friend must go to the Starfish Caves at the Southeast end of the island. There you will find The Great Nairb. Being not only the oldest, but also the wisest creature of this Great Earth. I shall be in need of his counsel."

Finally King Fiodoire turned to his beautiful wife " My Dearest you and I shall go together to gather all the residents of Mangdu. It is only proper that we make the Kitten feel welcome. With everyone's help, we can gather nuts and berries for a celebration feast. I am sure the goats will not mind sharing their milk with the kitten."

Pirsia steps forward quite anxiously and tells her father 'Um father, I uh... I'm not sure if I would know what this ...k i t t e n... looks like and I'm not sure if I'm the one who should go and bring her to you."

King Fiodoire could hear the fear in Pirsia's voice, he stepped forward brushing the hair out of her eyes and the gentlest voice reassured her, "Daughter have I ever given you reason for doubt or fear?'

With her head slightly bent Pirsia nodded and replied "Welll, no, but........"

"Listen my child, this kitten is a very gentle creature. She is lost and has much more reason to fear you. She will not harm you, that I can promise you. You will know when you've found her because she will have fur that is longer than yours and instead of hooves for feet she will have paws like the rabbits." King Fiodoire smiled as his daughter still reluctant to go stood in deep thought for just a few moments. Still not quite convinced but trusting her father she set off toward Sir Gahns' perch. Meanwhile the King and Queen became very busy with the help of all the residents on Timboura.

Pirsia reached the spot where the kitten was suppose to be. She approached very cautiously when she heard a strange noise. "Prrrrrr.. Prrrrr ...prrrrrr. Pirsia's eyes wide with fear now turned in the direction of the noise. Pirsia spots the large ball of fur sitting on a flower making the strange sound.

With extreme care she approached it and began walking around and around the fur ball on the flower. Thinking to herself this must be the kitten! The way it was moving. it seemed to be quite alive, but where was it breathing from? Pirsia studied the creature, it didn't have paws as father said, in fact it didn't seem to have eyes...........or a nose.........or any of the ordinary things one was used to seeing. It was just a huge ball of fur! Thinking the entire matter over very carefully Pirsia decides the creature certainly was not anything she wanted to be bother with. After all she had circled the silly thing three times now and it didn't seem to notice her.

Making up her mind not to bother the creature, Pirsia carefully backed away from the purring fur ball. Instead she tripped on a stone and fell forward, facing the kitten eye to eye.

Fluff stretched, looked into Pirsia's eyes and half yawning said "Are you King Fiodoire? King of Timboura?"

Totally forgetting her fear of the creature Pirsia laughs aloud " HA ha ha ha ha ha oohhhhhhhhhhh.............. nnoooo no no I am Princess Pirsia. King Fiodoire is my father. " Letting out one more giggle Pirsia explains " He sent me here to find you and bring you back to Mangdu."

"Mangdu? Who is that?" confused Fluff asks.

With another giggle Pirsia tells Fluff "Oh my, you are ever so funny.........Mangdu is not a who; it is our city, that is where we live."

" Ohhhh then you know Sir Gahn?" Fluff asked hopefully

"Yes kitten he will be waiting for us too."

Gaining the confidence of the kitten Pirsia leads Fluff out of the mushroom forest to Mangdu. As they entered the city they found every creature of the island gathered to greet their unexpected guest. For the children it was curiosity of seeing a cat or kitten for the first time in their lives. For the adults it was to see again another creature of the earth, that they sometimes remembered, but more often forgot about.

Dozens of seashells filled with nuts and fruit had been laid out in a large circle. There were also shells filled with milk, honey or nectar from fruit.; obviously a feast was at hand.

King Fiodoire announced "Citizens of Mangdu please feel free to welcome our guest, but do not over whelm her; I'm sure she is already a bit frightened. It seems she was left behind accidently by Old Drabu. Her story isn't long but a bit complicated. We must find the best solution for this lost kitten! As all of you know there are no others of her species on our island. I invite each of you to come forward if you have any suggestions.

Meanwhile enjoy the feast we have gathered here as we await our friend The Great Nairb to arrive. I hope all of you agree his wise counsel is surely needed at this time."

King Fiodoire looked at Fluff and saw her eyes wide with fear. In the gentlest voice he possible he told her "Do not be afraid little one, while many are staring at you, no one here shall harm you. My daughter Pirsia will stay at your side and I want you to meet Nivek. He will teach you things you need to know."

A short stout leprechaun stepped forward, bowed and said, "Hello Miss Fluff, that is your name is it not?" Fluff nodded and Nivek proceeded "The King has instructed me to tell you about the other parts of the world. Especially about humans."

"I'm not sure I want to know about humans, from what Sir Gahn told me............"

Before she could continue Nivek interrupted "What you heard was true enough, but you see your kind is loved by humans. Why all you have to do is let them love you and you need not fear them at all. Most of us here in Timboura were also loved by humans. The difference was we could grant wishes and do some magic. That caused greed to take over reason in humans Miss Fluff. You must realize that we citizens on Timboura are bound by custom, honor, love and duty to offer you a way home."

Dismayed Fluff told Nivek "How will you do that? I don't even know where home is, I don't know which direction to travel. Why I don't even know my mothers name!"

Thinking hard and scratching his beard Nivek replied " That is quite a dilemma little one, but rest assured The Great Nairb will know what is to be done for you."

"Nivek, what is a Nairb?"

"The Great Nairb is not a what but a who. He is the oldest creature alive on this whole Great Earth. No one knows more than The Great Nairb. He has seen and done more than anyone else. Despite his great age his memory is as sharp as a blade of grass."

Amazed Fluff asks "Do you think he will know where my home is?"

"That I cannot answer for you, but I do know that from him will come the wisest answera. Ah ......Here is The Great Nairb now. "

Nivek leaped up on a tulip, he began ringing a charming sound with a handful of seashells . Everyone stopped what they were doing and looked in his direction. "Listen! Listen, everyone our wise council The Great Nairb has arrived. His Majesty King Fiodoire has given me the honor of counseling our guest Miss Fluff about the earth and her creatures while Sir Gahn sits in counsel with The Great Nairb.

King Fiodoire is preparing to entertain us with a royal dance. For those of you who are very young and unfamiliar with this dance; it is performed only when we welcome a new creature to our island. The last time it was performed was about a hundred and fifty years ago when we welcomed Sir Gahn to Timboura."

Pirsia stepped forward and asked Nivek "What happened those many years ago Nivek, that Sir Gahn is still with us? From stories we've heard, we all know that most creatures of the Great Earth do not live as long as we do."

Nivek smiled at the wise little princess " That is true Pirsia, let me tell you all Sir Ghan's story briefly."

The day was a stormy one, Sir Gahn was a young fellow then, he quickly tired in the storm and soon drifted off of his course. Hours went by and totally exhausted he fell

into the Great Oceans. Being nowhere near land it was lucky for him; Ytram our friend the giant tortoise, and counselor to King Neptune saw him fall. Ytram knew he could not take him to the Coral City beneath the ocean; so instead Ytram brought him here to Timboura. King Fiodoire, Queen Modesta and The Great Nairb nursed him back to health.

As all of you know we have here in Timboura the much sought after and coveted Rainbow Fountain of Youth. As they nursed Sir Gahn back to health they of course used the water from the Rainbow Fountain. That is reason for Sir Gahns' longevity as well as our own. Since that time, Sir Gahn has become one of our most trusted and honored friends. After several weeks passed King Fiodoire and Queen Modesta performed the Royal Dance of the Unicorns to welcome Sir Gahn.

Tonight again we are honored to have with us Miss Fluff, she too will be welcomed in the same royal fashion that Sir Gahn was welcomed. His Royal Highness has indicated to me that they are ready for their audience. Every one quickly form a large circle so we can watch the royal performance.

With the circle formed around the royal couple, Queen Modesta stood regally with her head held high and proudly to one side . The King announced "My Queen and I will dance the "Unicorn's Welcome Rhapsody ."

Fiodoire slowly and gracefully bowed with one front leg bent and the other extended forward toward Modesta. With his head bent very low he began shaking his head slowly at first. Then faster and faster his head bobbed to and fro. Seashells and scales fastened to his mane made a very pleasant musical sound. Suddenly his head came up and he was on all four legs. King Fiodoire pranced around his Queen making her the center of his attention. Slowly and even more graceful than the King, Modesta stepped back with one front hoof, curtsied and she pranced toward her husband. With her hair gathered in flowers of many colors no sound came from her except the sound of her hoof beats. Dancing to the sounds The King was making, she came to a complete stop. Fiodoire leaped and pranced around her as she stood on her two back legs. As they danced for several minutes everyone was totally mesmerized. Then the dance ended with the Royal couple in the same position they had started their dance.

The applause of stomping hooves, clapping hands and whistling was almost deafening. Everyone was totally enchanted with the dance.

The King Stepped forward after the clapping subsided he announced "My fellow citizens, join me now one at a time to bid welcome to our lovely guest Miss Fluff. As you greet her and welcome her, I will council with my friends The Great Nairb and Sir Gahn to see what we might do for our guest. Enjoy the evening this is a night for celebration and enjoyment." The King Looked toward Fluff and Pirsia and added "After you have been greeted by all, the two of you should join in the festivities.

Pirsia stepped forward with Fluff to greet everyone, she proudly told them the bravery it took for her to bring the kitten to Mangdu. Everyone was enchanted and delighted to hear their stories and many chuckled at the silly fears each of the girls had encountered.

Time rolled by quickly and after several hours, King Fiodoire, The Great Nairb and Sir Gahn once again rang Nivek's seashells to get everyone's attention.

King Fiodoire began first "I regret that the information or conclusions we've came up with are quite limited Miss Fluff. I will let The Great Nairb fill you in."

The great Nairb rambled forward slowly and in a very deep echoing voice began "Many of you know the world out there is quite vast. Miss Fluff you must listen carefully to what I tell you. It would be improper of me to tell you, or even suggest that we could ever help you find your real home. However being a cat, you could have your home anywhere in the world even here in Timboura if you choose.

You are more fortunate than most of us, because your species is well loved and well taken care of by humans. Usually the smaller humans, the children thrive on your kind as pets. They can be capable of much love and adoration of their pet.

Thus, one of your choices is to remain here with us. We would welcome you and teach you our ways. Your only other choice is to go to the land of humans and see if you can find a family who will love and care for you. You need to remember that if you stay here, there are no others of your species here. While you are young it would not be so bad, however as you grow older into adulthood you would surely be lonely for one of your own kind to love. In the land of humans there would many others of your own kind to mingle with and who could relate to you in every capacity.

Should you decide to leave Timboura, my friend Ytram the giant tortoise can take you across the great oceans safely. Ytram's back is quite wide and warm, so your journey would be quite comfortable.

After several days Fluff made her decision to leave Timboura. The Great Nairb told her "You speak with much wisdom for one so young. Since this is your decision I think Nivek should be the one to tell you much more about humans. He can tell you what to expect of them, their habits and ways of life. You need to know that he, as well as the fairies are physically most like humans. Humans of course are much larger."

During the next few days Nivek told Fluff all he knew about humans and their habits. The more she learned she realized as she grew older she would want to be with as many of her own species as she could possible find.

During her instructions Fluff asked, " Nivek, how will I know when I've found a home I can call mine?"

Thinking long and hard the only answer Nivek had was, "Well, ... I would guess, that you will truly know you are home when they call you by your name. Yes, ...absolutely, I'm certain of it! I'm positive that when they call you by name; that is when you will know that you are home."

Finally the day came when Fluff was ready to leave. Queen Modesta and Princess Pirsia made sure Fluff had a large supply of goats milk so she would not go hungry. Every one on the island was at the beach to bid her a fond and happy farewell.

Ytram was happy and proud to be the one summoned to take Fluff across the oceans.

As they crossed the oceans, Ytram told Fluff what he knew about other parts of the world, and all about the weather. At times he just told her about his adventures at sea. As the two of them got nearer to the continent of North America the air got colder. Fluff huddled close to Ytrams' back.

Shivering Fluff chattered "I'm so cold Ytram!"

"Yes I know my dear ," Ytram said "Look over yonder in the direction we are headed. See all the white stuff falling? That is called snow. It is like rain, but frozen rain. See the land? Those very tall plants are called evergreens. See how they are covered with snow?"

"Oh yes Ytram, everything looks so beautiful and soft!" Fluff replied between chattering teeth.

"In this part of the world it is their winter season, as I told you about before. It is their coldest part of their year. As for being soft to touch it sometimes is soft but it can get very hard and icy. Winter is a very harsh season and it can be very dangerous. Fluff look straight ahead do you see that trail of gray climbing toward the sky?"

"Yes."

"That is called smoke, wherever you see smoke there are humans. They create the smoke with fire in their stoves or fireplaces. When I put you down on shore you must promise me, you will follow that smoke until you reach it."

"Oh, yes I promise Ytram."

"Listen to me very carefully little one; once you are off my back it will get much colder. The cold can kill you." Fluff listened somewhat fearfully "You must not stop for any reason until you've reached where the smoke is coming from. No matter how tired you are you must continue on, if you were to take a nap it would be the death of you. Many much larger than you have succumbed to the cold. You must not let the cold beat you"

"I.......... I promise Ytram."

Minutes later Ytram was on shore letting Fluff climb down his tail onto the snow covered beach.

"Remember little one, go toward that smoke and do not stop for any reason."

"Yes Sir th..... thank you f ...f ... for th ...the ride."

"One more thing little one, when you've reached the humans home you must scratch on their door and cry out as loudly as you can so that they know you are there."

"Okay........" Fluff turned away from the giant tortoise , not wanting him to see the tears and fear in her eyes. Fluff shivered, the cold winter air seemed to bite but Fluff began trudging toward the smoke "I must do this Ytram, ...bye ... I'll miss you." with that Fluff disappeared into a forest of trees.

Ytram watched for a little while and a tear went down his cheek as he realized he too would miss her. What a brave child, he thought as he swam back toward Timboura.

The wind in her face seemed to be mocking her, but Fluff trudged on. After more than an hour she could finally see the house of the human's. Totally exhausted Fluff fought her way against the wind and cold, she sat down for a moment. Shivering with extreme cold she pulled herself underneath a bush. The snow had not covered the ground as much there and it seemed to block out some of the menacing wind.

Fluff only meant to rest for a minute or two but little did she know the cold would make her so sleepy. Almost as soon as she was under the bush Fluff drifted off to asleep!

The wicked wind continued billowing more snow making it dance wildly against the already white earth.

So focused following the smoke Fluff had not seen the big gold bus, stopping at the end of the long narrow driveway. With the wind howling she also hadn't heard the little boy, calling out to her "Here kitty kitty………. here kitty."

Matt was sure he had seen the kitten drag herself under a bush.

Although only a few moments had passed it seemed like hours when an exhausted Fluff stirred, to the sound of a small raspy voice calling her "Kitty .... here kitty, come on kitty, ... here kitty kitty."

Fluff forced her eyes to open and she stared into very large green eyes and the funniest sight she'd laid eyes on. Fluff blinked and stared for a moment at the green eyes peering out at her through layers of cloth.

Woefully she cried out "MEEEEOW," she tried to purr but was shivering so much it was impossible. Instead she let out another Long "MEEEEOW!" Surely this is a human she thought. It was covered up with all kinds odd wraps as Nivek said they do. He had not told her they cover up everything even their faces. All she could see was this humans eyes staring at her. The human seemed to have lots of little brown dots all over its skin, she could not remember if Nivek had mentioned that or not. Having walked as far as she did in the cold she understood why they would want to cover up.

Once again the human called to Fluff "Here kitty kitty......come here kitty kitty." Shivering, tired and hungry, Fluff carefully got up walked over to the human letting out a long sad and soulful "MEEEEEOOOOOOW!" She remembered to rub her head against his leg as Nivek had showed her. She looked straight into his eyes and cried out a hungry "Meoooow."

"Oh you poor kitty. I'll bet you're hungry."

"Merrrrrrrroooow" Fluff answered

"What's your name girl? You sure are pretty. Do you belong to anyone? Are ya lost? Whatcha doing clear out here? Come on girl I'll take you inside. Betcha my mom'll let me keep ya. It's too cold for a little kitten like you to be out here wandering around in the snow." Matt reached down, scooped up the kitten and ran up the steps into the house.

"Mom, ...Mom."

"I'm in the kitchen Matt. Where's Diane?" Matt's mother replied.

"She's comin'. I ran ahead cause I saw this here kitty going under the bushes,..an she didn't believe me. I think she's hungry too!" As he enters the kitchen he lifts his hands filled with the cold, wet, furry, hungry kitten."

A very weak "meow" emerges from Fluff's mouth as she looks at the mother pathetically.

"Oh the poor dear, why it looks so tired. Surely she must be lost. This is a Persian kitten they are a very expensive breed; she must belong to someone." She put down a spatula she was

using and picked up Fluff. "Goodness the snow is stuck to her fur, she must be freezing......Hold on I think your sister just walked in. Diane is that you?"

"Yes mom it's me. Where's Matt? He said he saw something going....." Diane didn't finish her sentence, seeing her mother holding the kitten.

"Yes dear, he did, it's a very cold, lost and I would guess hungry kitten. Right now I'm going to get a large bowl of warm water and see if I can get this snow off of it's fur. Run upstairs and get me two big bath towels."

Diane did as her mother requested without hesitation. Then she and Matt watched as her mother gave Fluff a warm bath to melt away the snow embedded in her fur. Holding the cat wrapped in the towel, their mother carefully fed the kitten warm milk with a medicine dropper. The whole time she explained to them that the kitten was awfully small and there was a chance she might not make it. Fluff of course being more exhausted than hungry was soon fast asleep. Their mother carefully placed the kitten inside the dry blanket and laid her inside a laundry basket.

"Can I hold it mother?" Diane asked

"No," Matt yelled "It's my kitty and you didn't believe me!"

Their mother said sternly, "Matt there's no reason for you to yell at your sister like that. The kitten is tired and probably frightened, you're only going to scare the poor thing. It is no one's cat at the moment, if by chance she does not belong to anyone else, then maybe we can keep her and she will be *our* kitten."

As soon as their father came home they told him all about the kitten.

All through dinner their father said nothing regarding the kitten. Matt loaded the dishwasher while mother and Diane put away the leftovers. Father was putting the doily and bowl of fruit back on the center of the table when he broke his contemplative silence.

"Well,...." he began "It's true, she probably belongs to someone.....She's obviously a Persian. Since our closest neighbor is 4 miles from here she might be theirs. She might have fallen from a truck or car. It's odd that she's here, 17 miles from town. Even though the snow's stopped falling that wind is erasing any tracks she might have made to see which direction she came from." Everyone including mother listened intently and hopefully. "I think we should place an add in the local paper for thirty days to see if we can locate her owners."

Seeing the disappointment in Matthew's face, father asked him "If it was your kitten that was lost wouldn't you want someone to return it?"

Solemnly Matt answered "Yes sir ,........." he hesitated and then added "If no one claims her can we keep her?"

Diane and mother were as eager for father to say yes, the kitten was so sweet they had fallen in love with her immediately.

"Children you must understand, someone is more than likely to come forward, she is a very special and expensive kitten. I'm sure her owners are worried about her right this very minute. However if they do not come forward, then YES we can keep her."

They knew father was right but Diane spoke up next "Father do you think we should give her a name?"

Father responded "Right now let's just call her kitten or kitty."

Diane protested "But dad she might think that's her name."

"Diane," father said firmly "If .....and I do mean if, no one claims her, then I think she should pick her name."

"How will she do that father? "Matt asked confused.

"When and if that time comes I will explain. If the kitten already has a name her owner has given her, then our giving her another name would confuse her. So until then, I insist we all call her kitten or kitty.

The ad placed in the paper the next day read "FOUND, one very small kitten, about 17 miles north of Hardyville, call the Murphy's at 555-7779.

The thirty days passed excruciatingly slow. During that month only one person had called, but they were looking for a calico cat that was 7 years old.

Finally on the last day of the ad, father told them, "After supper we need to discuss the kitten."

During supper Matt remembered all the fun the kitten was during the thirty day waiting period. The kitten loved to chase him when she noticed he was in stocking feet and she always slept on his bed. The kitten loved to climb up on the ottoman father put his feet on, while he read the paper. Sometimes she would curl up on his knees and fall asleep. Father never seemed to mind. Mother would have to give her, her own ball of yarn to play with just so that she would leave mother's alone while she crocheted. Diane loved it when the kitten would climb up and lay in her lap and let her pet her endlessly.

After supper when everyone was settled in their favorite seat father began "I know you've all been waiting for this day to come but I have to remind all of you that her owner might still come forward and we would be obligated to return the kitten......." A dismayed look crossed everyone's face, but father continued "The likelihood however is pretty far fetched to worry about. We do have to remember she was lost. Now ....we need to give her a name."

Matt did not hesitate "Oh Father I think we should name her....."

Father cut him off before he could finish "Matt just hold on a minute, remember I told you she would be allowed to pick her own name......"

This time Diane interrupted "But Dad how can she......"

"Goodness me......" Father chuckled "Can a father finish what he's saying?"

Over excited, they all smiled and nodded realizing finally,it was certain they were going to keep the kitten.

Father continued "Okay Here's my plan........I'm sure we've all thought of a name for her; I think that we should each call her by the name we think best suits her and whichever name she responds most to will be her name. We'll each take our turn starting with mother then Diane, then Matt and then Myself. So follow me Gang, I'm sure she on her favorite sleeping spot,.... the foot of Matt's bed."

They followed Father to Matthew's room and sure enough there lay Fluff sound asleep.

Mother called out "Whitey, ... wake up Whitey, come on Whitey" Fluff awoke, stretched and yawned and looked at the mother puzzled. The mother called twice more, "Whitey come here Whitey."

The kitten only stared. Fluff wondered what they were doing and what the Mother was saying. She'd learned what 'come here' meant but this word 'Whitey' she'd never heard before.

The Father said "Go ahead Diane you try."

"Snowball, come here Snowball. Here Snowball" Fluff sat up and meowed at Diane

Fluff was trying to ask what they wanted ? What were the trying to say? They obviously wanted something but what?

Excited, Diane said did you see that Dad she sat up and meowed when I called her Snowball, I think she likes the name Snowball!"

"Yes, sweetheart I did see that she seemed to react to Snowball much more than Whitey, what do you think Matt?"

Reluctantly Matt admitted it "Awe gee Dad I guess so, ...but Fluff's a nice name too! It's true she is very white and when she's all curled up she kinda looks like a snowball but she's so fluffy I like the name Fluff.

Fluff couldn't believe her ears,............ Matt had said her name, ...she heard him!!! Not just once, but she heard him say it twice. He was talking to the father and using her name. She remembered that Nivek had told her "you will truly know you are home when they call you by name. All this time she had grown to love these humans, they played with her they cuddled her and fed her well. There were times she had feared that maybe this was not to be her real home. Sometimes she would be sad because they had not called her by her name. Now here stood Matt using her name while he talked to the Father.

Fluff jumped off the bed went over to Matt and cried "Meeeeerrrrrooooooow" ...... "Please, " she was trying to tell him "Please say my name again, call me by name.....please!!"

"What's the matter girl do you like the name Snowball?" Matt asked

More confused than ever Fluff just looked up at him.

Father smiled and gently said "Matt, try your name for her, it's only fair."

Matt looked down at the kitten he had rescued nearly five weeks before. He wondered what if the kitten would not respond to the name he'd picked? Almost afraid to say her name Matt called out softly "Fluff..."

There! He said it again Fluff's ears twitched and she began to purr "Prrrrrr, meow prrrrrrr"

"Fluff come here Fluff!" Matt almost sobbed, as he realized she was reacting to her name.

It was true, Fluff heard right! She rubbed her head into his legs purring and meowing with glee. She thought, I AM HOME!!! ALL THIS TIME I WAS HOME!!! Nivek was right!!!!!

Father put his arm around his son and said "Mathew I have a feeling that she like's her new name, ...Fluff, as well as her new home."

Printed in the United States
By Bookmasters